Mallory McDonald, Super Sitter

WORLD'S
BEST
BABY-
SITTER

For Becca and Adam

—L.B.F.

For Elliot and Juliette, who are both incredibly
creative and talented young artists.

—J.K.

Mallory McDonald, Super Sitter

by Laurie Friedman
illustrations by Jennifer Kalis

darby creek
MINNEAPOLIS

CONTENTS

A WORD FROM MALLORY

My name is Mallory McDonald, like the restaurant but no relation. I'm ten years old and in the fifth grade, and there are lots of things I like doing. I like to watch TV, draw, paint my toenails, bake cookies, spend time with my cat, and hang out with my friends.

There are also some things I don't like doing, such as washing lettuce and setting the table. That's what I did this afternoon, but I didn't really mind because I'm so excited about what's happening at my house tonight. The Goldmans, who just moved into the Winstons' old house next door, are coming for dinner along with Chloe Jennifer and her parents.

Even though Chloe Jennifer and I met the Goldmans when they moved in earlier this week, we don't know much about them aside from what we've seen—a mom, a dad, two identical twin boys, a blue minivan in the driveway, and newly planted pink flowers in the front yard.

When the Winstons moved out, I was sad that two of my best friends, Mary Ann and Joey, wouldn't be living on Wish Pond Road anymore. When I told Mom I was worried about a weird, mean, unfriendly family moving in, she told me that my imagination was running away from me.

I don't always agree with Mom, but this time, I think she was right.

Chloe Jennifer and I thought the Goldmans were really nice when we met them, and the twins were so, so, so cute! I'm excited to get to know them better and so is Chloe Jennifer. And the good news is that we don't have to wait any longer.

The doorbell just rang, which means dinner is served!

GIRLS TO THE RESCUE

"They're here!" I yell. Mom, Dad, and Max aren't far behind me as I run to the front door and open it.

Mr. and Mrs. Goldman are standing on our front porch along with their sons. It's almost impossible to tell the boys apart. They're identical in every way. They even have on matching striped shirts. The only difference is that one of them is holding a pretty bouquet of flowers.

Before we have a chance to find out who is who, the twin who isn't holding the flowers asks a question. "Are you the mom, or are *you* the mom?" He wags his finger back and forth between Mom and me like he's trying to determine who his brother should give the flowers to.

I can't help but laugh, and so does Max. "Lucas, don't be silly," says Mrs. Goldman. She points to Mom. "That's Mrs.

McDonald." Then she points to me. "And that's Mallory."

Lucas points to Mom. "Give the flowers to her," he says to his brother, who hands over the bouquet to Mom.

"Thank you," Mom says with a smile.

I can't tell if she's smiling because she likes the flowers or because she thinks it's cute that Lucas can't tell the difference between a mom and a ten-year-old girl. Then again, maybe he can tell, and he's just trying to be funny. I'm not sure which it is.

Either way, Lucas is adorable. He keeps talking. "I'm five," he says holding up a hand full of fingers.

"I'm Mallory," I tell him.

"And I'm Max," says my brother.

Lucas shakes his head at Max and me like we don't get what he's saying. "Five is how old I am, not my name. I'm Lucas." Then he points to his brother. "And that's Jared."

"Oh," I say like Max and I should have gotten it. As Max and I tell the boys how old we are, Chloe Jennifer and her parents walk up behind the Goldmans.

Can **YOU** tell them apart?

"Come in, everyone," says Mom.

When we get inside, the introductions start all over again with the Jackson-Browns. "How old are you?" Lucas asks Chloe Jennifer.

"I'm ten," she says with a giggle.

"What about you?" Lucas points to Chloe Jennifer's dad. Dr. Jackson-Brown laughs.

"Lucas!" Both his parents say his name at the same time and he jumps.

"You know you're not supposed to ask grown-ups how old they are," says Mrs. Goldman.

Lucas shrugs. "I forgot."

Max, Chloe Jennifer, and I all look at each other and burst out laughing.

But it's pretty obvious that Mrs. Goldman doesn't think Lucas is nearly as funny as we do. She takes both boys' hands. "I want you to remember your manners tonight. Can you do that?" she asks.

"*I* didn't do anything," says Jared.

Mrs. Goldman looks at both boys like she's waiting for a real answer. They both nod.

But as soon as we sit down for dinner,

Lucas blows milk bubbles through the straw in his glass and Jared tries to shove peas up his nose.

"Boys, no more silly business," says Mr. Goldman in a stern voice.

Both boys sit up straight, and they're good for the rest of the meal, but when we go to the living room for dessert, the trouble starts again.

"Is that a horse or a dog?" Lucas points to Champ, who is asleep on the floor.

Mrs. Goldman frowns. "I think you know the answer," she says.

"It's a horse!" screams Jared.

Lucas sits on Champ like he wants to ride him. "Giddyap!" he yells.

"That's enough!" says Mr. Goldman. He takes both boys by the hands. "I think it's time for us to go," he says.

Lucas and Jared look at each other. "We don't want to go," says Lucas.

"Please, can we stay?" Jared pouts like the idea of leaving is enough to make him cry. He has such a cute pouty face. It's hard to look away, but I turn my attention to Mr. and Mrs. Goldman.

"If you want to stay for a while and talk, we could take Lucas and Jared back to my room and play." I look at Chloe Jennifer, who nods like she likes the idea. "I don't know if they like to play with blocks, but I have a big bag of them. I could get them out."

"We love blocks!" says Lucas.

"Yeah! We want to stay and play," says Jared.

"PLEASE!" they say in unison.

"Are you sure you don't mind?" Mrs. Goldman asks Chloe Jennifer and me.

"I don't mind at all," I say.

"It'll be fun!" says Chloe Jennifer.

Lucas takes my hand and Jared grabs Chloe Jennifer's like everything has already been decided.

"OK," says Mrs. Goldman. "But only for a little while and, Mallory, please come get me if there are any problems."

"Don't worry!" I say over my shoulder as Chloe Jennifer, Lucas, Jared, and I head back to my room. When we get there, I get out the bag of blocks from the back corner of my closet.

"I used to love to play with these when I was your age," I tell the boys.

They look at each other and grin. "Can you build tall towers?" asks Jared.

I laugh. "I can build very tall towers," I say.

"Will you show us?" asks Lucas.

"Sure," I say.

Chloe Jennifer helps me stack block on top of block. When our tower is about a foot tall, Jared and Lucas start making funny noises. I look at Chloe Jennifer, and she shrugs like she's as confused as I am.

"What are you doing?" I ask the boys.

"We're starting our engines," says Jared. He and Lucas are on the floor on their hands and knees.

"We're bulldozers," says Lucas. "It's our job to knock down tall towers." He and Lucas crawl on all fours—straight into the tower Chloe Jennifer and I just built.

The blocks come crashing down around them, but they don't seem to mind. They're both on their backs cracking up.

Chloe Jennifer raises an eyebrow and gives me a *let's-play-along* look. I grin and nod. "Oh no!" says Chloe Jennifer. "Two bulldozers knocked over our tower."

"I guess we're going to have to rebuild it," I say. Chloe Jennifer and I start restacking the blocks.

Lucas and Jared eye each other. It's easy to tell this is a game they're going to like. As we build our tower, Lucas and Jared start their engines, and then they bulldoze our tower. "Oh no! It happened again," I say.

"We're just going to have to rebuild again," says Chloe Jennifer.

We keep building while Lucas and Jared keep bulldozing. When Mrs. Goldman comes to get the boys, they tell her they're bulldozers on a job and can't leave.

Mrs. Goldman looks at the tower Chloe Jennifer and I are building, and then smiles at us like she understands what we've done to keep the boys entertained.

"Why don't you bulldoze this last tower," Mrs. Goldman says to her sons. "I'm sure those nice builders are going to have to call it a day."

"That's right," I say out loud. "This is our last tower tonight. We're all finished." I place the final block on the tower. Chloe Jennifer and I stand back as the boys knock the blocks to the ground.

"Girls, I can't thank you enough," says

Mrs. Goldman. Then she motions to the blocks scattered all over my floor. "Boys, please help clean up," she says.

While Lucas and Jared put the blocks back into the bag, Mrs. Goldman adds, "You girls did a great job keeping the boys entertained." When the boys are done putting away the blocks, she puts one arm around Jared and the other around Lucas.

"Do we really have to go?" Lucas asks.

"We had fun," says Jared.

"So did we," says Chloe Jennifer. She smiles at Lucas and Jared.

"Maybe we can play another time," I say to the boys.

They give their mother a hopeful look. She nods like she likes the idea too and then smiles at Chloe Jennifer and me.

"We'll just have to see what we can do about that," says Mrs. Goldman.

A PROPOSITION

When I walk into the kitchen after
school, Mom and Mrs. Goldman are
sitting at the table drinking coffee.
"Mallory, I have a proposition for you,"
says Mrs. Goldman.

I feel like I'm at school, and I have no
idea what one of my vocabulary words
means. "What's a proposition?" I ask.

Mrs. Goldman smiles like my question is
a good one. Then she pulls out her phone

and starts reading. "The definition of a proposition is a suggested plan of action, especially in a business context," she says.

"You want to do business with me?" I ask, surprised.

Mom smiles. "Actually, she would like to do business with you and Chloe Jennifer. Why don't you see if Chloe Jennifer can come over so Mrs. Goldman can explain her idea to both of you at the same time?"

"Sure," I get my phone out of my backpack and text Chloe Jennifer.

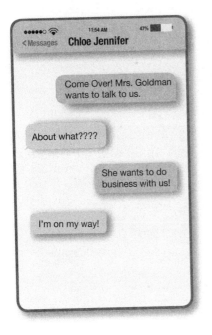

Then I wait outside on my front porch for Chloe Jennifer. "What do you think she wants to talk to us about?" she asks as she walks up.

"I don't know," I say.

"You don't think we did anything wrong when we were playing with Lucas and Jared the other night, do you?" she asks.

I shake my head. "I don't think she'd want to do business with us if we did."

"That's true," says Chloe Jennifer.

When we go inside and sit down at the table with Mom and Mrs. Goldman, we find out we did things right, not wrong. "Girls, the other night Lucas and Jared had a wonderful time playing with you," says Mrs. Goldman. "We had fun too," I say.

Chloe Jennifer nods in agreement.

Mrs. Goldman smiles. "I'm glad to hear that." She pauses. "I'm a writer. I work from home, and I have a deadline coming up. I have a lot of work to do over the next few weeks."

Mrs. Goldman takes a sip of her coffee and continues. "I was planning to hire a babysitter to watch the boys in the afternoon when they come home from school. I had someone older in mind, but the boys had such a good time with the two of you, I decided to see if you would be interested in the job."

Chloe Jennifer and I give each other a *being-babysitters-would-be-fun* look.

"Before you decide if you'd like the job, let me tell you a little more about what I have in mind," says Mrs. Goldman.

Chloe Jennifer and I listen carefully as Mrs. Goldman talks.

"The job would start immediately. I'd want you girls to come over tomorrow after school. I'll stay with you and the boys for the first few days. It will be like a trial run. If that works, I'd like to hire you

for three weeks to take care of the boys while I write."

I glance at Mom. She gives me a little nod like she approves of what she's heard so far.

Mrs. Goldman keeps talking. "Since I work from home, I'll be just down the hall if you need me. Your hours would be from three thirty to five thirty, five days a week, and I'll pay you each $2.50 an hour."

Mrs. Goldman pauses. When she starts

talking again, her voice sounds more serious. "It will be your job to keep the boys occupied and safe while I work."

"Think carefully before you answer," says Mom. "Babysitting is a big responsibility."

Chloe Jennifer and I look at each other and nod. I want to do it, and I can tell she does too. "I'm in," I say.

"Me too," says Chloe Jennifer. "You can count on us."

"We'll take good care of Lucas and Jared," I add.

Mrs. Goldman looks happy. "Wonderful! They'll be thrilled when I tell them." Then she stands like it's time for her to go. "I'll see you tomorrow afternoon."

We say good-bye to Mrs. Goldman and thank her. We wait until she's gone, and then we break out in a happy dance. "We're going to be babysitters!" I scream.

Chloe Jennifer and I join hands and jump around in a circle.

"I can't wait to tell everyone at school," says Chloe Jennifer.

Mom laughs as we jump around chanting "We're babysitters!"

When we finally stop jumping and chanting, Mom looks at us. "Girls, I'm delighted you have this opportunity. But it won't be all fun and games. Babysitting can be hard work."

"I'm not worried," I tell Mom.

How hard can it be?

OFF TO
A GOOD START

"Chloe Jennifer and I have some big news," I say as I sit down at the lunch table between April and Mary Ann. I raise a brow at Chloe Jennifer, who is sitting across from me, and give her a *do-you-want-to-tell-them-or-should-I?* look.

Chloe Jennifer clears her throat. "Mallory and I got hired to be babysitters." Everyone at the table listens as she tells them about Lucas and Jared and how Mrs. Goldman hired us to watch them while she works. "We start this afternoon," she says.

Mary Ann frowns. "It's kind of weird that you'll be babysitting in my old house."

I hadn't thought about that. I guess I get why she would think it's weird, but I'm still excited. "At least we'll know our way around," I say with a smile.

Mary Ann shrugs. "I don't know," she says. "Every afternoon is a lot. I wouldn't want to do it."

"I think it's cool," says April. "I'd love to babysit."

"Me too," says Pamela. "Little kids are really cute."

"Right?" I say. I'm glad April and Pamela get why babysitting is going to be fun.

But Arielle shakes her head like she doesn't agree. "Not all little kids are cute."

Chloe Jennifer and I exchange looks as Arielle talks about all the annoying things her five-year-old cousin, Amanda, did when she came to visit with her family last summer and slept in Arielle's room.

"I don't want to sound mean," says Arielle. "But I was happy when she left."

"Well, Lucas and Jared aren't annoying," I say as I think about how much fun we had after dinner the other night.

"Anyway, *we* wouldn't have time to babysit," Danielle says as she looks at Arielle. "We're too busy with dance."

Arielle nods in agreement.

"I think babysitting is cool, if that's what you're into," says Zoe, like it's her turn to give an opinion since she's the only one who hasn't said anything. "Babysitting wouldn't be my thing. I'm into learning to play the guitar."

"That's cool," I say and take a bite out of my apple. But as Zoe starts to talk about her guitar lessons, I think about what my friends said. I didn't expect so many of them to say babysitting won't be fun.

I thought they'd be as excited about our new job as Chloe Jennifer and I are.

After lunch, in math class, I try to focus on fractions, but my brain is busy thinking about what my friends said.

Just because some of them said they wouldn't want to babysit doesn't mean Chloe Jennifer and I won't like doing it. At least, I hope it doesn't mean that.

I don't even know why I'm thinking about

what they said. Before I talked to them, I was super excited. I try to push everything else out of my brain and go back to being as excited as I was before I talked to them.

When school is over for the day, Chloe Jennifer and I meet outside the school gates and start walking back to Wish Pond Road.

As we walk, we talk about what happened at lunch. "Did it bother you that Mary Ann, Zoe, Arielle, and Danielle didn't think babysitting would be fun?" I asked.

Chloe Jennifer shrugs. "Everyone is into different things. It didn't bother me that some people weren't as excited about babysitting as we are. I think it's going to be great!" she says with a smile.

"Me too!" I say as we walk up to the Goldmans' house.

"I guess it's time to find out," say Chloe Jennifer as she pushes the Goldmans' doorbell. We hear footsteps running to the door. Chloe Jennifer and I grin at each other.

"Welcome!" says Mrs. Goldman when she opens the door.

"You're here!" screams one of the boys, grabbing my hand.

"Are you Lucas or Jared?" I ask.

Both boys laugh. The one who's not holding my hand takes Chloe Jennifer's. "Guess," he says.

Chloe Jennifer and I look from boy to boy. It's impossible to tell them apart. The only difference is one of them has on a red shirt and one of them is wearing a blue one.

Mrs. Goldman clucks her tongue like she disapproves, but it's easy to see that she's not really mad. "Don't give Mallory and Chloe Jennifer a hard time on their first day. Tell them how they can tell who is who."

One of the boys points to the other.

"I'm Jared and that's Lucas. You can tell us apart because he's more bad than I am."

"No, I'm not," Lucas says and bops Jared on the head.

Mrs. Goldman ignores their exchange. "You can tell them apart because Jared likes to wear his watch."

Jared grins. "We got Superman watches for our birthday. I wear mine every day." Then he points to his brother. "But Lucas never wears his."

"So you're Jared who likes his watch."

Jared nods. I high-five him. "Got it."

Mrs. Goldman smiles. "Now that we have who's who out of the way, we'll show you where we like to play."

"Lead the way," says Chloe Jennifer as we follow an excited Lucas and Jared into the house.

"Wow!" I say when we get to the family room. There are toys and games everywhere. "There's plenty to do here. What's your favorite game?" I ask the boys.

Lucas gets out Twister. As we start to play, Mrs. Goldman sits down on the sofa with her laptop and starts typing. When Jared gets too twisted, he falls down and Lucas jumps on top of him. They both start laughing. Mrs. Goldman looks up and smiles.

When we're done with Twister, the boys want to do puzzles. Lucas and Jared each do a puzzle.

"Wow! You're both awesome at puzzles," says Chloe Jennifer.

Lucas and Jared grin at each other. "Yeah, but we stink at cleaning them up. You're the babysitter. That's your job."

Mrs. Goldman looks up. I wait for her to tell the boys to clean up, but she doesn't. Chloe Jennifer and I give each other a *this-is-a-test* look.

"Let's see who's better at it," I say.

"Whoever does the best job putting his puzzle away neatly gets to decide what we do next," says Chloe Jennifer.

Jared and Lucas don't wait for us to say Go. They both start filling the boxes with puzzle pieces.

Mrs. Goldman nods at us like she approves.

Lucas finishes putting his puzzle away first, but Jared isn't far behind. "That was really close," I say when they're both done. "What do you say we do another puzzle and when you're both through, we'll see who can put theirs away first."

The boys scramble to get out more puzzles. They do puzzle after puzzle and compete to see who can put them away fastest for the rest of the afternoon. Mrs. Goldman works on her laptop. She looks up occasionally and smiles. When it's time for us to go, Mrs. Goldman closes her laptop. "Boys, Mallory and Chloe Jennifer have to go now," she says.

"We don't want you to go!" says Lucas.

"Yeah," says Jared. "We're still playing."

Mrs. Goldman smiles sympathetically. "They'll be back tomorrow," she says.

"YAY!" scream Lucas and Jared at the same time. They take our hands and walk us to the door with their mother.

"See you tomorrow," I say.

"Bye," says Chloe Jennifer.

"Bye, girls—and thanks very much," says Mrs. Goldman. "You did a great job today." When she closes the door, Chloe Jennifer and I high-five each other.

We're off to a good start!

RHYME TIME

"Students, your attention, please!"

Mrs. Finney, our principal, waits at the podium in the auditorium for the Fern Falls Elementary fifth and sixth graders to quiet down.

"This morning, I'm going to share with you the details of a special new program at school." She pauses like she's waiting for a drumroll. "I'm proud to announce the first-ever Fern Falls Elementary Poetry Slam," she says.

The auditorium gets noisy again.

"What's a poetry slam?" I ask Pamela, who is sitting next to me. But before she has time to answer, Mrs. Finney explains.

"A poetry slam is a competitive event in which poets perform their work." Mrs. Finney pauses and lets her explanation sink in.

"Participants will write and present a poem on the topic of their choice. You can be as dramatic as you'd like when you present your poem, but no props or costumes are allowed. It's a good idea to choose a topic that is personal and important to you so that the emotion you feel will come through naturally when you present your poem."

My brain starts searching for topics. Maybe I'll write a poem about Cheeseburger. My cat is very important to me.

Mrs. Finney keeps talking. "The poetry slam is only open to fifth and sixth graders. You may present your poem solo, or you may enter as a pair."

Mrs. Finney glances down at some papers on the podium. "In three weeks, we're going to have a special evening program where our poets can present their work. There will be a panel of judges to give scores to the participants and award prizes for the winners. Parents and families will be invited to attend."

Everyone around me starts talking about entering and how cool it would be to win a prize.

Mrs. Finney clears her throat. "The real benefit of a poetry slam comes from being able to see the poet, hear his or her words, and feel the emotion of the poem. The audience will connect with you if you perform your poem from the heart."

Mrs. Finney ignores the giggles from the students in the back row. I get why kids are laughing. What she said sounds kind of silly, but I actually like the idea. I listen as she keeps talking.

"Registration details are posted on the

bulletin board outside the gym. I hope you'll all consider participating," says Mrs. Finney. Then she dismisses us to go to our next class.

Some kids might think a poetry slam is dumb, but I think it's cool. "Are you going to enter?" Pamela asks as we leave the auditorium.

"I'd like to," I say. I love to write poetry, and it would be great to win a prize. But it's one thing to write poems no one sees and a whole other thing to present one of my poems onstage.

"I just have to figure out what I'm going to write about," I tell Pamela. I don't think any of the poems I've already written are good enough for a contest like this, and I don't think writing about Cheeseburger is exciting either.

Pamela nods like she gets why it's important to find a good topic. "I definitely want to enter. I'm thinking about writing my poem about playing the violin. Do you think that sounds boring?"

"Not if you write a poem about how exciting playing the violin is," I say.

Pamela laughs and then shakes her head like that wasn't what she had in mind. "I was thinking I might write about how it can be scary to play in a competition."

"That sounds like a really good idea," I say to Pamela.

We wave as we split up to go to our

classes. I think about the poetry slam during social studies and even during PE. I try to think of a topic. Then I think about who I could enter with. It sounds like fun to do a poem with someone else.

I'm going to ask Mary Ann if she wants to be my partner. There are so many fun things we've done together that we could write about.

At lunch, everyone at my table is talking about the poetry slam. "Danielle and I already signed up," says Arielle. "We're going to do a poem about dancing. It's going to be about how we've been dancing together since we were four years old."

"That sounds cute," says April.

"Zoe and I already signed up too," Mary Ann announces to the table.

Zoe nods and picks up where Mary Ann left off. "We're going to present a poem about how healthy eating can be nutritious and delicious."

"Good idea," says Pamela.

"Yeah, I like that," says Chloe Jennifer.

I don't say anything. I can't believe Mary Ann already picked Zoe to be her partner. I know they're both into healthy eating. They've been spending a lot of time together lately. But still, it would have been nice if Mary Ann had asked *me* if I wanted to do a poem with her.

I look around the table. The only people who don't have partners are April and Chloe Jennifer. I'm going to see if either of them is interested. As we leave lunch, I catch up to April. "Do you think you're going to enter the poetry slam?" I ask.

April laughs. "No way," she says. "I always get scared onstage."

"What if we did it together? It wouldn't be as scary if you were onstage with another person."

"I'm really not interested," says April.

When I ask Chloe Jennifer, her response is no better than April's. "Sorry, Mallory, I just don't have time. I have dance and piano lessons, plus we're babysitting."

"I know," I say. "But it will be fun."

Chloe Jennifer shakes her head like she won't change her mind. I really want to find someone to enter the poetry slam

The Girl without a Partner.

Do you want to be my partner?	Not me.
Or me.	Or us.

with. In science class, I ask Joey if he wants to enter with me.

"I already signed up. I'm going to do a poem about skateboarding," he says.

Then I ask Devon if he wants to enter with me. We made such a good team when

we did our book report together that I
think he might say yes. But he's planning
on doing a poem with one of his five
brothers, who happens to be in sixth grade.

I can't believe every single person I
asked to be my partner said no. I would like
to have a partner. But I also really want
to enter the poetry slam, even if I have to
do it alone. I just have to figure out what I
want to write about.

Luckily, I have plenty of time for that.

HIGHS & WOES

When the week started, Chloe Jennifer and I were super excited. Last week, we passed our babysitting test with flying colors. At least that's what Mrs. Goldman said.

We babysat Lucas and Jared three afternoons last week while Mrs. Goldman stayed around and watched. At the end of the third day, Mrs. Goldman said we had earned an A+ in babysitting. And she wasn't the only one who thought we had done a good job.

Lucas and Jared told us we were the best babysitters they've ever had. They actually started cheering when their mom said we were coming back.

That was a week ago. Now, it's Friday again and all I can say is that I'm glad this week is over. Maybe my friends who thought babysitting wasn't a good idea were right. The job has turned out to be a lot harder than I thought it would be.

Lucas and Jared weren't nearly as good when their mother wasn't watching. Plus, it was hard to babysit every afternoon AND find time to do all my schoolwork.

This has been a really tough week. If you don't believe me, keep reading and you'll see what I mean.

MONDAY

When Chloe Jennifer and I showed up at the Goldmans' house on Monday, I said that the boys were so good that our job should be easy. Mrs. Goldman laughed and warned me not to let my guard down. "The boys are not always good," she said.

And she was right. As soon as Mrs. Goldman went to her office to work, Lucas and Jared went to hide. They didn't say anything like, "Let's play hide-and-seek." Or "We'll hide and you find us." They just hid. And we couldn't find them!

We looked everywhere. We were starting to get worried we wouldn't be able to find them. "Maybe we should tell Mrs. Goldman they're missing," said Chloe Jennifer.

"We can't do that," I said. "We're

responsible for them! And they have to be here somewhere."

We kept looking for them. We finally found them, but we looked for twenty-seven minutes before we did.

"We love to hide!" said Jared when we finally found them in the storage closet in the laundry room.

"Do we get the award for best hiders?" asked Lucas.

"No award!" I said.

"We were worried," Chloe Jennifer told Lucas and Jared.

We waited for them to say they were sorry, but as they high-fived each other, they didn't seem sorry at all.

TUESDAY

On Tuesday, Lucas and Jared wanted to play chase in the backyard. The game was pretty simple: they would run and we would chase them. Once we caught them, they'd run and we'd chase them again.

We played chase for a long time. Chloe Jennifer and I were getting hot and tired and sweaty. "Why don't we play a different game," I said to the boys.

When I said that, Lucas whispered something in Jared's ear. "OK, we have a different game," said Lucas. Then, before he told me what the game was, he and Jared climbed up the big tree in the backyard. Once they got high up in the tree, they said they were too scared to climb down. They wanted us to climb up and help them down.

They didn't look scared, but they couldn't stay up there forever. We finally climbed up and helped them even though we knew they didn't really need help climbing down. But all the chasing and the climbing made me extra tired. When I got home from babysitting, I sat down at my desk to do my homework. But instead of doing homework, I fell asleep!

And that's where Mom found me. She told me it was time for dinner. I ate dinner, and I knew that after dinner, it was *really* time for me to do my homework. But I was too tired, so I just went straight to bed.

WEDNESDAY

On Wednesday morning, I woke up early to do the homework that I hadn't done Tuesday night. I got it all done, but when I got to school, I got more homework that I was supposed to do Wednesday night.

I was wondering how I was going to babysit after school and do my homework at night. I didn't think I could do it all, and then I found out I had even more to do.

Mr. Moreno assigned a project in social studies. "I want each of you to build Abraham Lincoln's log cabin," he said. He gave us all a picture of it so that we would have something to use as a guide.

I raised my hand. "Do you want us to build this tonight?" I asked.

Mr. Moreno laughed. "No, you have two weeks to build it."

As Mr. Moreno talked about what we

have to do, all I could think about was that even though I was relieved the project wasn't due tomorrow, I still had a cabin to build.

THURSDAY

Thursday was the worst day of the week. At school, everyone was talking about the poetry slam. "Mallory, are you going to enter?" asked Pamela. "I didn't see your name on the list."

I told Pamela I wanted to enter it. The only problem was that I hadn't had any time to think about what I would write about.

I decided I would think about it that night, but when we got to the Goldmans' house to babysit, Lucas and Jared wanted to skate outside. They put on their skates and skated on the sidewalk all along Wish Pond Road. Since Chloe Jennifer and I didn't have skates (only sneakers), all we could do was chase them while they skated.

They skated for two hours while we ran after them, which meant that when I got home, I was tired and grumpy and the last thing I wanted to do

was my homework (which I had a lot of) or think about a topic for my poem.

FRIDAY

Now it's Friday, and today was no better than the rest of the week.

When we babysat, Jared karate-chopped my leg. I asked Lucas to get me some ice to put on my leg (which hurt from being karate-chopped). But instead of getting ice, he got a glass of ice water. And instead of giving it to me, he spilled it on me.

He said it was an accident. But I was soaking wet, and Lucas and Jared couldn't stop laughing. It didn't seem like an accident.

"I'm not so sure I'm glad we agreed to be babysitters," I said to Chloe Jennifer as we left the Goldmans' house.

"This was our first week," she said. "It will probably take time for us to get used

Nothing is funnier than a wet babysitter!

to it—and for the boys to get used to us."

"It's not just that," I said. "I haven't had enough time to do my homework. And I haven't started my project or thought of a topic for the poetry slam."

"The good news is that it's Friday and you have the whole weekend to work on those things," said Chloe Jennifer.

"I guess you're right," I said.

Chloe Jennifer linked her arm through mine and smiled. I know she was trying to cheer me up. But I'll feel cheerier when I've done everything I need to do.

A SURPRISE VISITOR

"SURPRISE!"

When I walk into the kitchen, I can't believe what I see. Grandma is sitting at the kitchen table with Mom. "Grandma!" I scream. I run to her and give her a big hug. "I didn't know you were coming to Fern Falls."

"I wasn't doing anything this weekend," says Grandma. "So I decided to pop in for a quick visit and check on my Honey Bee."

I smile. That's the nickname that Grandma has been calling me for as long as I can remember, and I love it. "I'm always happy to see you, Grandma."

She pats the chair next to her, and I sit down. "Your mom was just telling me there's a new Chinese restaurant in town," she says. "You know how much I love Chinese food. We thought it would be fun to give it a try tonight."

"That sounds great," I say.

"And tomorrow, your parents are taking Max to his baseball-pitching clinic, so I thought you and I could spend the day together."

I raise a brow. If Mom and Dad are going to be gone all day tomorrow with Max, I suspect that Mom called Grandma to come to take care of me. "Grandma, are you going to be my babysitter?" I ask.

Grandma laughs. "If taking you out to lunch and to see a movie sounds like babysitting, then that makes me guilty as charged."

Now it's my turn to laugh. "I didn't know it was possible for a person to be a babysitter *and* need to be babysat."

Grandma looks at me like she doesn't understand what I'm talking about.

"You're not the only babysitter in this house," I explain to Grandma. I tell her about babysitting for Lucas and Jared.

"What a fabulous opportunity," says Grandma. "How's it going?"

Mom looks at me like she's just as curious to hear my answer as Grandma. I pause before I say anything. "Babysitting is a lot harder than I thought it would be," I tell them. That's an honest answer, but it's not the whole answer.

What I don't tell them is that because I've spent so much time babysitting, I haven't had enough time to do my schoolwork or start my project or work on my poem.

If I tell them I have so many things to do, I know they'll both say that going out to lunch and to a movie tomorrow is a bad idea, and I really want to go. I make a silent promise that I will work on finding a topic for my poem on Sunday.

I, Mallory McDonald, do Solemnly Swear...

And I don't forget that promise I made. When Sunday rolls around, I grab a notebook, a pen, and Cheeseburger and go into the kitchen.

Mom, Dad, and Max are already at the table, and Grandma is at the stove making blueberry pancakes. "How about some pancakes, Honey Bee?" she says when I sit down.

I fill a glass with orange juice. "I always like your pancakes," I say. "But what I'd really like is some help." I tell Grandma about the poetry slam at school. "I wanted to enter with a partner," I tell her. "But I couldn't find anyone who wanted to do it with me."

"I would be your partner if I could," says Grandma. Just picturing myself presenting a poem with Grandma at the poetry slam makes me smile.

"I know you can't be my partner," I say as I help myself to a pancake. "But maybe you can help me come up with an interesting topic to write about." I look at Mom, Dad, and Max. "You can help too," I tell my family.

Grandma sits down at the table with a cup of coffee. "I think it's always best to write about something you're interested in," she says.

That sounds a lot like what Mrs. Finney said. "Our principal told us we should choose a topic that's personal and important so that the emotion comes through when we present our poems. That's what I'm trying to do, but I'm having a hard time deciding what to write about," I say.

Dad puts a pancake and some fruit on his plate. "You could write about your wonderful, loving parents," he says.

"That's a great idea! I'm sure you could write a lovely poem about us," Mom says. She winks at me as she pours syrup on top of her pancakes.

"I'm sure I could," I say. I know Mom and Dad are just joking around. I appreciate their humor, but picking a topic for my poem is no laughing matter.

"I want to write about an activity I'm interested in," I say.

Max stuffs his mouth full of pancakes. "If I wrote a poem, it would be about baseball."

"Max, please don't talk with your mouth full," says Mom.

I roll my eyes at my brother as he piles two more pancakes and some bacon on his plate. I remind him that he's supposed to be helping me.

"Didn't you take an art class this summer?" asks Grandma.

"You also planted a garden with Mrs. Black," Mom reminds me.

Dad gets up and pours himself another

cup of coffee. "I think drawing and gardening are excellent topics for a poem," he says.

"I don't know," I say. Even though drawing and gardening are good topics, I don't feel excited about the idea of writing a poem about either of them. "I think I'm having a hard time picking a topic because I really want my poem to be good," I say.

Grandma walks over to my chair and puts her hand on my shoulder. "Honey Bee, I know you'll think of something."

"When?" I ask.

Grandma bends down and kisses me on the forehead. "An idea will pop into your head, and you'll know when you've found the right topic."

"You really think so?" I ask.

"I know so," said Grandma.

I hope she's right.

TOO MUCH TO DO

I learned something new at school today. What I learned is that I have a math test this Friday and a science test next Monday. In addition to that, I have to turn in my log cabin next Tuesday, and I haven't even started it yet.

I have so much to do that I don't see how I'm going to get it all done.

"I think I'm going to quit babysitting,"

I tell Chloe Jennifer as we leave the Goldmans' house.

Chloe Jennifer sucks in her breath. "Mrs. Goldman hired us to watch Lucas and Jared for three weeks while she works. It's only Wednesday. We still have two more days this week and all of next week." She pauses and looks at me. "You can't quit. We agreed to do this together. We're a team."

"I know," I say. "But when I agreed to do it, I didn't know how busy I would be at school."

Chloe Jennifer frowns. "Is this about what happened with the pudding yesterday? You know it was an accident."

When Jared dropped his bowl on the floor, pudding splattered everywhere. Lucas tried to help clean it up—at least he *said* he was trying to help—but when he did, it made an even bigger mess. Chloe

Jennifer and I had to clean up the kitchen *and* the boys. It wasn't fun, but it's not why I'm quitting.

"It's not about that," I say. "I just have too much to do."

Chloe Jennifer shakes her head at me. "That's not a reason to quit," she says.

Actually, I think it's just one reason why I should quit, and I can think of lots of others. When I get home, I write them all down and then I show them to someone who I know will agree with me.

I walk into the kitchen and hand Mom the list I made. "You need to read this," I say. I stand beside her while she reads.

Mom finishes reading and hands me back my list. I wait for her to say I can quit. But that's not what she says.

"Mallory, you made a commitment and Mrs. Goldman is counting on you."

"I know," I say. "But I don't have time to babysit *and* do everything I have to do for school."

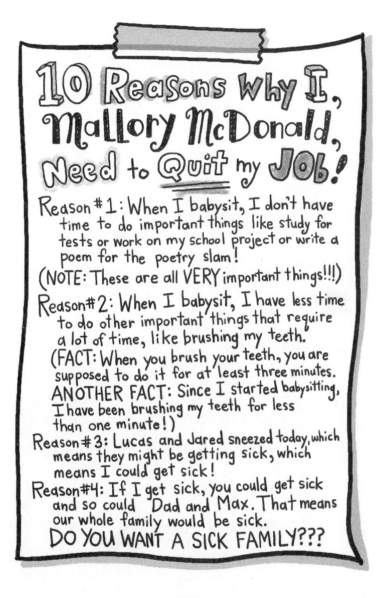

10 Reasons why I, Mallory McDonald, Need to <u>Quit</u> my JOB!

Reason #1: When I babysit, I don't have time to do important things like study for tests or work on my school project or write a poem for the poetry slam!

(NOTE: These are all VERY important things!!!)

Reason #2: When I babysit, I have less time to do other important things that require a lot of time, like brushing my teeth.

(FACT: When you brush your teeth, you are supposed to do it for at least three minutes. ANOTHER FACT: Since I started babysitting, I have been brushing my teeth for less than one minute!)

Reason #3: Lucas and Jared sneezed today, which means they might be getting sick, which means I could get sick!

Reason #4: If I get sick, you could get sick and so could Dad and Max. That means our whole family would be sick.

DO YOU WANT A SICK FAMILY???

Reason #5: If everyone in our family is sick, who will take care of Cheeseburger and Champ? OUR PETS ARE OUR RESPONSIBILITY!

Reason #6: Sometimes when I babysit, I get frustrated. Frustrated people say bad words. I NEVER say bad words, but if I keep babysitting, I might say one. Do you want me to say a bad word????

Reason #7: If I say a bad word, Lucas and Jared (WHO ARE ONLY FIVE!) might hear me say it. Do you really want them to hear a bad word?

Reason #8: If I quit my job, I will have time to do things you might want me to do like clean up my room. (You have wanted me to do that for a long time!)

Reason #9: If I'm not babysitting two hours a day, I can use those two hours to sleep more. Children grow when they sleep. Don't you want me to grow?

Reason #10: If I sleep more, I will be more pleasant. Sleepy people are unpleasant. THIS IS A FACT. Don't you want me to be a more pleasant person?

I NEED TO QUIT MY JOB!

"You can't just quit," says Mom. "It's important to finish what you start. You need to make a schedule so that you have enough time to get everything done."

Mom takes a piece of paper from the desk and tells me to sit down at the table. She asks me exactly what I have to do and when everything is due, and we make a schedule. "If you follow this, you should have plenty of time to get everything done."

It wasn't the answer I was hoping for, but maybe Mom is right. "I'll try," I say.

I go to my room and spend the rest of the evening studying for my math test. I study again on Thursday night. On Friday, I'm ready for my test.

On Saturday, I study for my science test. While I'm studying, Mom sticks her head in my room. "How's it going?" she asks.

"Great!" I say. The schedule Mom and I made is actually working.

But Saturday night, things go from *great* to *not so great*. My family goes to the Winstons' house for dinner, and Joey and Mary Ann start talking about the poetry slam.

"We worked on our poems all day today," says Mary Ann.

"Have you written a poem yet?" asks Joey.

"Not yet," I say like it's not a big deal. But just listening to Joey and Mary Ann talk about their poems, which they've already written, makes me feel like it's a very big deal that I don't even have a topic yet.

I know Grandma said that an idea would come to me, but it hasn't yet. Trying to pick a topic is on my list to do tomorrow. I'm going to brainstorm ideas

for my poem in the morning and work on my project in the afternoon.

When Sunday arrives, I make a list of topics for the poetry slam. But it's hard for me to choose one. I'm not sure which topic would be the most exciting. I text my friends to see if they can help me choose.

But my friends aren't much help.

When Max's girlfriend, Sam, comes over after lunch, I decide to read my list

Which topic do you like best for my poem: Cheeseburger, gardening, art???

Mary Ann: Cheesburger!

Joey: Gardening!

Pamela: Art!

of topics to them. "Can you help me choose?" I ask.

But when I ask for their help, Sam gives Max a funny look. "We were going to ask if you want to go with us on a bike ride."

I'm so surprised that my mouth almost drops open. Max has never asked me to do something fun with him and a friend. I really want to go, but I also need to pick a topic and work on my project.

"Maybe getting some fresh air will help you choose a topic," adds Sam.

I hadn't thought about it like that, but it

makes sense. Grandma said I would know when the right idea comes to me. Even though I have a lot of work to do, maybe a change of scene is all I need to help me decide what I want to write about, and when I get back, I'll work on my project.

"I'd love to go," I tell Max and Sam.

Then I make a solemn promise. It sounds a lot like the promise I made last weekend.

The only difference is that this time I really mean it.

I, Mallory McDonald, do solemnly promise that the minute I come back from the bike ride, I will start working on my project.

That's a promise I intend to keep.

A BREAKDOWN

When my alarm rings, I turn it off and stretch. Waking up is usually one of my least favorite times of the day. But today, I'm excited to get out of bed.

When I went biking yesterday with Max and Sam, I decided to write my poem about our ride. We had a lot of fun racing up and down hills. Now I have fresh material to write about.

And when I got back, I worked really

hard on my log cabin project. I didn't finish until late last night, but Mom wasn't mad. She thought my project turned out great, and so did I.

The **House** Where **Abe** Lived.

Built by Mallory. | My house never looked so good!

And the best news is that even though my project isn't due until tomorrow, I'm going to turn it in today. That means I'll have time to write my poem tonight.

I throw on clothes and brush my teeth and hair. When I get to the kitchen, I put food in Cheeseburger's bowl and gulp down a glass of milk. Then I go to the laundry room to get my project.

But when I walk into the laundry room, I'm shocked at what I see.

My project doesn't look anything like the log cabin I made last night. In fact, it doesn't even look like a log cabin. It's just a pile of brown-painted Popsicle sticks and a big square piece of Styrofoam.

"Mom! Dad! Come quick," I yell.

Mom, Dad, and even Max are in the laundry room faster than an Olympic athlete can run the fifty-yard dash. "Mallory, are you OK?" asks Mom.

I point to the pile of sticks on top of the washing machine. "Look what happened to my log cabin," I moan. "The logs came unglued!"

"It's a BREAKDOWN," says Max.

"Max!" Mom gives him a *now-would-be-a-good-time-to-keep-your-mouth-shut* look.

"Let's see what's going on," says Dad.

I pick up one of the Popsicle sticks. Just looking at the mess on top of the washing machine makes me feel like I'm going to throw up.

I painted all those sticks and glued them all to the Styrofoam. I even made a little chimney, and a door and windows, and I put a sign in the front yard.

Mom, Dad, and Max gather around my project to inspect it to see what went wrong.

"Maybe the paint on the sticks was still wet when you glued them on," says Mom.

Dad shakes his head like he doesn't think that's the problem. "I think maybe the glue you used doesn't work on Styrofoam," says Dad.

"Maybe you're just a bad cabin builder," says Max.

"MAX!" Both my parents say my brother's name at the same time.

"Sorry," he says before my parents have a chance to tell him he's in trouble for making me feel worse than I already did. Then he leaves the laundry room like it's not somewhere he wants to be.

I feel tears starting to form in the corners of my eyes.

"Mallory, show me the tube of glue you used," says Dad.

I get the tube of glue out of the cabinet over the dryer and hand it to Dad. He starts reading the teeny, tiny instructions on the back of the tube.

I don't see how reading those directions is going to solve my problem. My problem is that the project I worked so hard on is in shambles.

"What am I going to do?" I moan.

"Your project isn't due until tomorrow, right?" asks Mom.

I nod.

"You can redo it tonight," says Dad. "Instead of using a Styrofoam square, you can use a small cardboard box. The sticks will adhere much better to cardboard. I can even bring home some extra-strong glue to be sure they stick."

I know Dad is trying to be helpful and make me feel better, but I don't. A tear rolls down my cheek.

"It took me a lot of time last night to build the cabin. I don't have time to do it again tonight. I'm babysitting this afternoon, and I was planning to work on my poem tonight." I wipe my eye on my sleeve.

Mom looks like she feels badly for me. "I'm sorry, Mallory. But you're going to have to redo your project tonight."

"When am I going to write my poem?" I ask.

"You'll have to work on it tomorrow night," says Mom.

"The poetry slam is on Friday, and

that doesn't leave much time for me to rehearse it and be ready." My head is throbbing. Even though I know I'm not sick with any kind of virus, I feel sick about what happened to my project.

Dad wraps an arm around me. "Sweet Potato, sometimes things happen that you don't expect. When they do, you just have

to accept that you have a problem and do what you need to do to fix it."

Dad looks me in the eye. "Can you do that?" he asks.

"I guess I can," I say.

It's not like I have a choice.

DOUBLE TROUBLE!

Today was officially a mostly bad day at school.

Not because of anything that happened. I just couldn't stop thinking about my ruined project. And it didn't help that everyone else was talking about the poetry slam this Friday.

"Zoe and I spent all day yesterday rehearsing," Mary Ann said in homeroom.

"Yeah," said Zoe. "We're totally ready."

"That's great," I said. And it is great. For them. But it didn't make me feel better.

At lunch, the conversation about the poetry slam continued. Pamela said she finished her poem, and Arielle and Danielle said they were done too.

"Can we talk about something besides the poetry slam?" asked April.

I get why she didn't want to hear any more about it. She's not entering it. I didn't want to hear any more about it either, but that's because every time someone said something, it reminded me that I still hadn't written my poem.

The only good news is that when I got to math class, Mr. Hudson said we could use class as a study hall since we had a test on Friday. I decided to use it to start writing my poem. I wrote a few lines about the bike ride I went on with Sam and Max.

Three bikers go on a ride one day.

With the wind on their backs, they fly away.

When class was over, I put my notebook away. I was happy with what I'd written. I just wish I'd had time to write more.

"You're very quiet," says Chloe Jennifer as we walk from school to the Goldmans' house.

"Yeah," I say. "I'm just thinking about my

poem." I'm still thinking about it when we get to the Goldmans' house.

"Can we do artwork inside?" Jared asks Chloe Jennifer and me when we arrive.

Lucas crosses his arms across his chest. "I want to play outside," he says.

Chloe Jennifer looks at me. "Why don't we split up?" she says. I'll take Lucas outside to play, and you can sit with Jared in the kitchen while he colors."

"I like that plan," says Jared.

"Me too!" says Lucas. He grabs Chloe Jennifer's hand and pulls her toward the backyard.

"I guess it's you and me," I say to Jared. And I'm glad about that. I take a stack of paper and a bucket of crayons from the art cabinet in the laundry room and set him up at the kitchen table. "You can draw here," I tell him.

I sit down at the table, pull out my notebook, and keep working on the poem I started in study hall.

They pedal hard, down the street.
They pedal fast. They use their feet!

While I write, Jared colors. This is working out great. If Jared keeps coloring, I can finish my poem this afternoon and work on my project tonight.

"Mallory, do you like my picture?" Jared asks.

I look up. Jared shows me his drawing. "Is that your family?"

Jared nods.

I study the picture. "You're a really good artist," I say. "I bet one day you'll be a real artist with artwork that hangs on walls everywhere."

"How do you get to be a real artist?" Jared asks.

"You have to practice," I tell him. I think about the poem I'm writing. I need to get back to it. "Why don't you draw another picture?"

"OK," says Jared. "Can I use markers this time?"

"Sure," I say.

Jared goes to the laundry room to get the markers while I keep writing.

Down hills, the bikers go.
Uphill is slow, slow, slow.

I think my words sound very poetic. I scratch my head as I try to think of more lines. But suddenly, I realize Jared isn't back from the laundry room. It shouldn't have taken him that long to get the markers.

I walk into the laundry room. But there's no sign of Jared. I go back into the kitchen and check his bedroom. But Jared isn't in either room. He seemed pretty excited to draw, but he could have changed his mind. I know how much he likes to hide.

I check his favorite hiding spots. But he's not in the living room behind the couch or in the hallway closet next to the dining room.

When I go into the family room, I see Jared, but he's not hiding.

I gasp. I can't believe what I'm seeing. Jared is standing on a table behind the couch, using his markers to color on the wall. All over the wall!

I grab Jared and pull him down. "What are you doing?" I ask as I take a fat red marker out of his hand.

"I'm making real art," he says.

When I said Jared would have art on walls, I didn't mean the walls in this house!

Mrs. Goldman is going to be so mad when she sees what he's done.

I have no idea what to do. I take Jared by his arm and lead him outside. "Go play with Lucas," I say, pointing to the swing set.

Then I talk to Chloe Jennifer. "We have a problem," I say. I tell her what Jared did in the family room while I was in the kitchen. When I finish telling her what happened, I wait for her to help me figure out what we're going to do about it.

But that's not what she does.

"How could you let that happen?" she asks me.

I don't see how she could think this is my fault. "Jared knows better than to color on the walls," I say.

"Mallory, you were supposed to be watching him, not working on your poem."

A minute ago, I was mad at Jared for

coloring on the wall. Now I'm mad at Chloe Jennifer. I remind her what happened to my project this morning.

But Chloe Jennifer doesn't seem to care about my project. "Mallory, we made a commitment to babysit!" she says.

"When I said I'd babysit I didn't know other things like a poetry slam and a school project were going to take up a bunch of

Simmering Sitters

my time. And I had no idea that I'd do my project and then have to redo it," I say.

"But keeping the boys out of trouble is more important than any of that!" says Chloe Jennifer.

"Well, if you hadn't suggested that we split up, this wouldn't have happened."

She gasps. "What happened was NOT my fault!"

While we're arguing about whose fault it is, we hear a thud. Then we hear a scream. A loud scream! And we're not the only ones who hear it.

Mrs. Goldman runs into the backyard. "What happened?" she asks.

"My knee!" moans Lucas.

There's blood everywhere.

"They were talking about something, and they weren't watching us," says Jared pointing to Chloe Jennifer and me. "Lucas tried to fly off the tower and he crashed."

Mrs. Goldman looks at us like we have some explaining to do. Then she scoops up Lucas. "Let's get this knee cleaned up," she says.

Chloe Jennifer and I look at each other as we follow Mrs. Goldman to the kitchen. She only knows half the story, and she's not going to be too happy when she finds out the other half. Unfortunately, it doesn't take her long to find out.

On the way to the kitchen, she walks through the family room. When she sees the wall that Jared colored on, she stops. "What happened here?"

She doesn't even wait for an explanation. She carries Lucas into the kitchen, sets him down on the counter next to the sink, and turns on the water.

"Ouch!" screams Lucas when she puts soap on his knee. He starts crying again as she washes it off.

Chloe Jennifer and I just stand there while she bandages his knee. When she's done, she turns toward us like she's waiting for an explanation.

Chloe Jennifer looks at me like it's up to me to tell Mrs. Goldman what went wrong. I take a deep breath. Then I tell her everything.

I tell her that Jared and I were at the table and he was coloring. I tell her that when he went to get the markers, I got distracted writing my poem and that when I realized he wasn't back at the table, it was too late.

I tell her that I went outside, and that when Chloe Jennifer and I were talking about what happened, we weren't watching Lucas and Jared, and that's when Lucas fell.

"I'm really sorry," I say to Mrs. Goldman.

"So am I," says Chloe Jennifer. I know she blames me for what happened in the family room. I get it. I should have been watching Jared. But I think she's apologizing because she's just as responsible as I am for not paying attention to Lucas and for letting him fall.

Mrs. Goldman is quiet for a minute before she speaks. When she does, her voice is very low, like she's mad and doing her best not to show it.

"Girls, I appreciate your apology. But I hired you to watch the boys, not to do your schoolwork or stand around and talk to each other. It is time for you to go."

"You don't want us to babysit anymore?" I ask.

"What about your deadline?" asks Chloe Jennifer.

Mrs. Goldman doesn't answer our questions. She opens her purse, gives us each some money, and then she walks us to the front door.

I think Chloe Jennifer and I just set a new world record.

Youngest people to ever be fired.

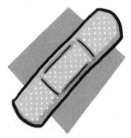

MAD PEOPLE

A Story by Mallory McDonald

Once upon a time there was a sweet, smart, cute redheaded girl with freckles who got hired to babysit cute twin boys with one of her best friends.

She thought babysitting would be a lot of fun.

She NEVER thought that it would end up with a lot of people being mad at her, but that's exactly what happened.

This afternoon, a LOT of people got mad at her.

The first person who got mad at her was her friend who was babysitting with her.

The sweet, smart, cute redheaded girl with freckles told her friend that one of the little boys had colored on the wall while she wasn't watching. Her friend got mad and said it was the redheaded girl's fault.

They started to argue about it, and when they did, something else happened.

The other little boy (not the one who colored on the walls) fell. He started screaming and crying that he was hurt.

And that's when another person got mad.

The person who got mad was the boys' mother.

At first, she was just upset that her son was hurt. But when she found out

Mad Person #2

what happened in the family room, she got even madder.

The redheaded girl apologized. She felt terrible. She hoped the mom would say something like: That's OK. I forgive you. But that's not what she said.

The mom told the girl (and her friend, who was already mad) that she would not be needing them anymore and that they could go home.

The girl didn't think her friend could be any madder than she had been, but she was. She said all kinds of mad things to the redheaded girl.

The girl had never seen her friend get so mad. Usually her friend was nice and calm and understanding. But she didn't seem to understand that the redheaded girl was sorry for what had happened. The redheaded girl kept trying to apologize. She felt really, really, really bad. She hoped her friend would say something like It's OK. I forgive you. It's kind of my fault too.

But the friend just went home to her own house.

I can't believe what happened! I got fired from my first job! Because of you!

The sweet, smart, cute redheaded girl with freckles felt just awful. Her friend was mad. The boy's mother was mad. She didn't think there was anyone else who could be mad at her.

But she was wrong.

When she got home, her mother was waiting at the door and she did not look happy.

She told the girl that the mother of the

Mad Person #3

boys who she supposed to be babysitting called and told her what happened. The girl's mom said that the girl took on an important responsibility and did not take it seriously. She said that the girl did not prioritize or manage her time well. She said that she was very disappointed in her because they had talked about how important it is to finish something that you start and that the girl did not do that.

The girl tried to explain that when she started babysitting, she didn't know other things were going to get in the way and make it so hard to finish.

She told her mother she did what any girl in her position would do.

She tried to multitask, and that's when the problems started.

She thought her mother would understand what she was saying and be proud of her for being a multitasker.

But she wasn't.

She told the girl that when you make a commitment to do something and people are depending on you, you have to follow through, and that part of growing up is learning to accept responsibility.

mul·ti·task·ing (noun)
the handling of more than one task at the same time by a single person

The girl reminded her mother that she wasn't fully grown up yet and that maybe her mother should start treating her like she's ten and not seventeen.

The girl was surprised (in a good way) when her mother agreed that that was exactly what she should do. But then she sent the girl to her room to think about what she'd done. She said that was an age-appropriate thing for the girl to be doing.

So that's where the girl is now. In her room, thinking about what she did.

And trying to figure out if there's something she can do to fix things.

But she hasn't thought of anything yet (and she's been thinking for a while).

Poor girl.
THE END

Girl in her room, thinking

HAPPY FACES

I push the doorbell and wait. After everything that happened yesterday, I'm pretty nervous about what's going to happen today.

Lucas and Jared look at each other. "You're back!" says Lucas.

They look surprised to see us, and I don't blame them. I didn't think Chloe Jennifer and I would be back at the Goldmans' house to babysit either.

But last night when Mom sent me to my room to think, it actually worked.

I thought of a plan to fix things, and when I told her about it, she thought it was a good one. The next person I talked to was Chloe Jennifer. First, I sent her a text.

I'm soooo sorry about what happened.

It was my fault too.

Sorry I blamed it all on you.

Can we talk?

YES!

So I called Chloe Jennifer and explained my plan to her. She liked it a lot. So we went to the Goldmans' house and tried out our plan on Mrs. Goldman.

This makes it sound like I came up with a complicated scheme—like something a spy might do in a movie when he has to get out of a bad situation.

But it wasn't anything like that. My plan was a pretty simple three-step plan.

STEP #1: Chloe Jennifer and I admitted we made a mistake.

STEP #2: We apologized.

STEP #3: We asked for another chance.

When we finished, Mrs. Goldman smiled. It looked like our plan was working!

We also offered to paint the wall that Lucas colored on, and we told Mrs. Goldman that we would babysit for free for the rest of the week.

Mrs. Goldman told us the marker would wash off the wall and that she would give us another chance. When Mrs. Goldman agreed to let us try again, Chloe Jennifer added that we could also make a schedule of activities for each day, so that we would always have a plan for what we would do with the boys.

I promised Mrs. Goldman that we would be the best babysitters ever. And that's a promise Chloe Jennifer and I both intend to keep.

Jared tugs on my shirt like it's time for me to pay attention to him. "What are we going to do today?" he asks.

Chloe Jennifer and I smile at each other, and I reach into my pocket and pull out the schedule we worked on last night.

"We've got a lot to do!" Chloe Jennifer says to Lucas and Jared. "First up, healthy snacks!" Chloe Jennifer opens up a loaf of bread and puts a slice of bread on two plates. I get out the peanut butter, raisins, bananas, and honey.

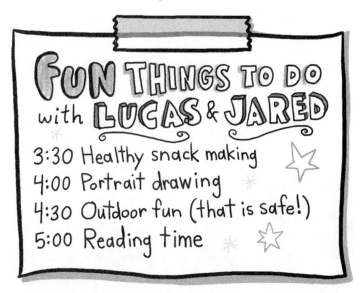

FUN THINGS TO DO with LUCAS & JARED

3:30 Healthy snack making
4:00 Portrait drawing
4:30 Outdoor fun (that is safe!)
5:00 Reading time

"Today, we're making smiley-face sandwiches," I say.

Chloe Jennifer and I help Lucas and Jared spread peanut butter on their bread. Then we show them how they can use raisins, banana slices, and honey to make the eyes, nose, and mouth. "Be creative when you make your sandwich!" I say.

Jared uses bananas for eyes, raisins for a nose, and a squirt of honey for the mouth.

"Can I use grapes for the eyes, a baby tomato for the nose, and pickles for the mouth?" asks Lucas.

"Are you sure you like tomatoes with peanut butter?" I ask.

Jared makes a face. "That sounds yucky."

I kind of think so too, but apparently Lucas doesn't. "That's what I like."

"You can put anything on your sandwich as long as you eat it," says Chloe Jennifer as she gets the grapes, tomatoes, and pickles out of the refrigerator.

"Good job being creative," I say to Lucas as he puts on the finishing touches. Both boys' sandwiches look very happy, and so do the boys as they eat them.

When the boys are done eating their sandwiches, we ask them to help us put away everything in the kitchen. Then we get out art supplies and spread them out on the kitchen table.

"Today we're going to draw portraits," I tell Lucas and Jared.

I look at Jared. "On paper!" I say.

Jared nods like he gets it. I'm sure he does. I know he got into a lot of trouble for coloring on the walls, and I don't think it's something he'll do again.

"What's a portrait?" asks Lucas.

"Good question," I say. "It's a picture you draw of a person. Or if you want to draw a picture of yourself, it's called a self-portrait."

"I want to draw a picture of you," Lucas says to me.

"And I'm drawing one of you," Jared says to Chloe Jennifer.

We sit and watch while they both draw us. When they're done, they show us their pictures.

Chloe Jennifer and I both smile when we see out portraits. Jared's picture of Chloe Jennifer isn't bad. The portrait

Lucas drew doesn't look like me at all. But it's obvious both boys had a lot of fun drawing them.

When we're done drawing, we take beach towels and go outside. "Today, we're going to teach you how to do yoga," says Chloe Jennifer.

She shows the boys how to do the Downward Dog pose.

"Who taught you how to do that?" Jared asks as he gets into the pose.

"My mom does yoga, and she taught me," says Chloe Jennifer. Once both boys master that pose, she demonstrates how to do the Triangle pose and then the Warrior pose.

While she's showing them how to do a Cat and Cow Stretch, Mrs. Goldman comes outside to watch.

"You boys are real yogis," she says with a laugh. The boys are all smiles as they show their mom the other poses we taught them.

I've never been so glad to see so many happy faces.

Finally, Chloe Jennifer and I read part of one of Lucas and Jared's favorite books, a Captain Underpants story, out loud to them. Then it's time for us to go.

"Will you be back tomorrow?" Jared asks. He and Lucas look at their mom like they want to be sure we're coming back.

Mrs. Goldman looks at us and nods. "Yes," she says. "I'm happy to say that Mallory and Chloe Jennifer will be back."

We're happy too. As we leave, we talk about how well the day went. "Making a schedule of activities was a great idea," I say to Chloe Jennifer.

"Thanks," she says. "But I wouldn't have thought of it if *you* hadn't had the idea to ask Mrs. Goldman for another chance. I feel like we've learned a lot about babysitting."

When she says that, it gives me another great idea. A really great idea!

"We should do the poetry slam together," I say. "I know you said you don't have time. But you're right. We've learned so much about babysitting. I think we could write a really great poem about it."

"But haven't you already written a poem?" she asks.

I remember what Grandma said about an idea popping into my head and knowing when I've found the right topic. Something tells me I've found it. "I don't mind starting over," I say.

Chloe Jennifer smiles. "I love that idea!" says Chloe Jennifer. But then her smile turns into a frown. "But how are we going to do it in time?" she asks. "The poetry slam is on Friday, and we're babysitting after school all week."

I learned the hard way that multitasking isn't always a good idea. "We'll have to work on the poem *after* we're done babysitting," I say.

Chloe Jennifer laughs. "Another great idea," she says.

"Want to start now?" I ask.

Chloe Jennifer nods, and we high-five as we walk into my house together.

We've got a poem to write and not much time to write it.

A POETRY SLAM

"It's time!" Chloe Jennifer whispers as we wait backstage with all the participants in the poetry slam.

"Welcome to the first-ever Fern Falls Elementary Fifth- and Sixth-Grade Poetry Slam," we hear Mrs. Finney say to the audience.

"Are you nervous?" whispers Mary Ann, who is sitting in a chair beside me.

I look around the area backstage, which

is filled with fifth and sixth graders who are participating in the slam. "A little bit," I say.

But the truth is that I'm *very* nervous.

Chloe Jennifer and I were up late last night putting the final touches on our poem. We didn't have time to rehearse again this afternoon because we had to babysit. It was our last day, and when we left, Mrs. Goldman told us we did a great job. I just hope we do as well when it's our turn to go onstage.

I turn my attention to Mrs. Finney, who is explaining to the audience how the poetry slam will work.

"Participants will be presenting individually or in groups of two," explains Mrs. Finney. "They will have three minutes each to present their poem. We have a panel of three judges who will be evaluating the presentations, and at the end, we will announce a winner and three runners-up."

I peek at the stage and the audience through the divide in the curtains. I know Mom, Dad, and Max came, and so did the Goldmans. When Chloe Jennifer and I told Mrs. Goldman what our poem is about, she said that they'd love to come. I try to see if the auditorium is filled, but it's hard to tell from backstage.

"Now I'd like to introduce our judges,"

says Mrs. Finney. The panel is made up of Ms. Martinez, an English teacher at Fern Falls Middle School, Mr. Cobb, the first-grade teacher at Fern Falls Elementary—who is a poet himself and has had poems published in magazines—and Mrs. Denson, the drama teacher at the middle school.

I'm happy when I hear her name. "She was the director of the play I was in last year," I whisper to Chloe Jennifer. She squeezes my hand like it's a good thing that we know someone on the panel.

I hope Mrs. Denson will give us a good score. I feel like we can use all the help we can get.

"The last thing I'd like to say before we get started is that you, the audience, are welcomed and encouraged to express yourselves," says Mrs. Finney. "If you like something, feel free to clap, snap your fingers, or whistle. Just no foot stomping, booing, or tomato throwing."

Everyone laughs when she says that.

Mrs. Finney waits for the laughter to die down and then says, "Now it's time for the Fern Falls Elementary Poetry Slam to begin!"

I feel like I'm at the starting line of a race. There are a lot of poets, and I really hope Chloe Jennifer and I finish first.

The Race of the Poets!

Ready, set, go! | The poets are off!

Mrs. Finney calls the first presenter up. It's a girl in sixth grade who presents a poem about horses. I can't see her, but

I can hear her, and what I hear sounds pretty boring. But it doesn't seem like the audience agrees with me, because when she's done, there's lots of clapping and finger snapping.

Next up are two sixth-grade boys who present a poem on football. I'm not a big football fan, but I know enough about the sport to know that when they present their poem, they sound like the announcers on TV.

When they finish, the crowd screams and yells. It kind of feels like we're at a football game and not a poetry slam. Knowing they did such a good job makes me feel even more nervous as Chloe Jennifer and I wait for our turn.

We sit through six more poems, and then it's Joey's turn. "Good luck," I say as he walks up to the stage.

His poem is about the thrill of skateboarding. I'm not the only one who thinks his presentation is thrilling. The audience goes crazy clapping, cheering, and whistling. When he comes backstage, I give him a thumbs-up.

There are more poems on a variety of topics. Some of them are funny, and some are more serious.

When Devon and his brother present a poem about having the same size feet and how their socks are always getting mixed up, the audience cracks up.

A sixth-grade girl presents a poem about her dog that died, and it makes me cry.

Pamela presents her poem about how scared she gets at violin competitions, and then Mary Ann and Zoe present their poem about healthy eating. Arielle and Danielle actually dance when they do their poem about dance. We can hear their feet tapping onstage.

Each time one of my friends finishes a poem, I clap. I didn't think any of their poems were as good as the one the girl did about her dog or the one Devon and his brother did. Still, they all did a good job and I'm happy for them.

There are two more presentations, and then it's our turn. Chloe Jennifer squeezes my hand hard as we get up from our seats. "My stomach is doing flip-flops," she whispers.

"Mine too," I say. I'm tense, but I'm also excited.

We walk out to the stage. I look out across the auditorium. The judges are at a table in front of the stage. The auditorium is packed, but the lights are bright and it's hard to make out individual faces.

Mrs. Finney gives us the sign that it's
time to begin, and Chloe Jennifer starts.

Babysitting is what we do.
Every day it's something new.
We play games. We read books.
Sometimes we get dirty looks.

When she says that, we both make
faces, just the way we practiced. The
audience laughs, which is what we hoped

they'd do. I wait for the laughter to die down, and then I take a deep breath and pick up where Chloe Jennifer leaves off.

Some days we want to quit.
Other days we'd like to forget.
But we still like what we do.
Because we get to take care of two.

I pause, and Chloe Jennifer starts again.

We babysit twins. They're the best.
Even though we never get to rest.
They love to run and jump and play.
We have fun with them every day.

I'm just about to start reading the last part of our poem, but before I do, someone else has something to say. "Hey, they're talking about us," screams

Lucas. He and Jared stand on their chairs and start waving their arms.

"We're the twins they babysit for," Jared says pointing to us.

"But we're not babies," says Lucas. When he says that, the audience goes crazy, laughing and clapping. Jared and Lucas take bows from their seats.

I finish our poem. But it's not easy to do over all the noise.

Double the trouble means double the fun.
We're sad our babysitting job is done.

Chloe Jennifer and I both make sad faces, and the crowd claps and cheers. When we go backstage, everyone tells us we did a great job. As the final contestants present their poems, it's hard to focus on their poems. I'm thinking about the judges.

136

I hope they think we did well too.

When all the poems have been presented, Mrs. Finney goes back out to the microphone and asks all the poets to please join her onstage. "Let's give a big round of applause to all our poets," she says.

"Now the moment you've all been waiting for," says Mrs. Finney. The auditorium gets quiet. Mrs. Finney asks the judges for the envelope with the names of the winners.

The runners-up are Devon and his brother, Arielle and Danielle, and a sixth-grade boy who presented a poem about how many times he has broken his arm.

"Do you think we won?" Chloe Jennifer whispers to me as Mrs. Finney gives a book of poems to each of the runners-up.

"I don't know, but we're about to find out!" I point to Mrs. Finney, who is back at the microphone.

"I'd now like to announce the winner of the first-ever Fern Falls Elementary Poetry Slam." She pauses. "Actually, there are two winners. It was a tie."

The first winner is the girl who presented the poem about her dog who died. I'm not surprised. Her poem was really good. Chloe Jennifer and I squeeze hands.

"The other winner of the Poetry Slam is Joey Winston," says Mrs. Finney.

The audience claps and cheers as Mrs. Finney gives the winners their prizes. They each get a book of poetry and a writing journal. I'm happy for Joey, but as Chloe Jennifer and I walk together to the reception in the lobby of the auditorium, I can't help feeling a little disappointed that we didn't win. It would have been fun to get a prize.

But my sadness doesn't last long.

"Mallory!" screams Lucas.

"Chloe Jennifer," screams Jared.

They run up to us and give us big hugs. "We're famous!" says Lucas.

It's hard to be upset about not winning when they tell us how excited they were that our poem was about them. Plus, it feels good to know that we were the only presenters who had audience participation.

Mr. and Mrs. Goldman walk up, and Mom, Dad, and Max join our group too. Everyone tells Chloe Jennifer and me what a good job we did.

"I knew you were good babysitters," says Mrs. Goldman. "But I had no idea you were also good poets."

"Thanks," I tell Mrs. Goldman. Then I grin at Lucas and Jared. "We had some good material to write about."

"We think you and Chloe Jennifer should have won," says Jared.

"Yeah," says Lucas. "The other poems were boring." He fake yawns like they almost put him to sleep.

Everyone laughs, and then Mrs. Goldman takes both boys' hands. "Speaking of sleep, it's time for us to go home and go to bed. It's late."

"I'm not tired," says Lucas.

"Neither am I," says Jared.

"You might not be tired," I say. "But I sure am!"

As I drive home with Mom, Dad, and Max, I think about my bed and my cat. I'm excited to curl up with Cheeseburger. It has been a long day.

But a good one!

REST & RELAXATION

As soon as I wake up, I look at the clock on my nightstand. It's already nine o'clock. I usually sleep in on Saturdays, but I never sleep this late. Last night was a big night, though. And I guess I'm tired from more than just the poetry slam. I've had a busy week.

I pull Cheeseburger closer to me and close my eyes. As soon as I do, someone knocks on my door. It's Mom. "Good morning, sleepyhead." She sits down on the edge of my bed.

I roll over so my back is toward Mom. "I'm so tired," I say as I yawn.

Mom rubs my back. "You've had quite a week," she says. "What you need is some R & R."

I sit up and look at Mom. "What's R & R?" I ask.

She laughs. "Rest and relaxation."

I smile and then I pat my rumbling tummy. "Some rest and relaxation sounds nice, but I'd like to start with some breakfast."

Mom laughs. "I think that's an excellent idea."

I scoop up Cheeseburger and follow Mom down the hall to the kitchen. Max and Dad are already at the table.

"How's my poet?" Dad asks.

I get a glass and fill it with orange juice. "Dad, I'm not just a poet," I say. "A poetry slam is about what you say *and* about how you say it."

Dad puts down his coffee cup. "You are absolutely right." Then he winks at me. "How's my daughter who did an excellent job at the poetry slam last night?"

I take a sip of juice and then smile like I appreciate the compliment. "I'm very tired from all my activities this week," I say. Then I yawn and make an *ahhh* sound as I stretch. "I'm planning on getting some R & R today."

Max rolls his eyes like I'm being dramatic.

Dad laughs. "I think that's an excellent

idea. How do you plan to rest and relax?"

I hadn't thought about what I'm going to do. "Well," I say slowly, "I'll take Cheeseburger for a walk this morning. Then I'll call my friends." I really want to hear what Mary Ann and April and Pamela and Joey thought about the poetry slam. "Then I think I'll make myself a healthy lunch."

"That sounds nice," says Dad.

"I'm not done," I say.

Mom and Dad look at each other and smile.

I keep talking. "I'm also going to call Grandma. I want to tell her about what happened with Lucas and Jared and about the poetry slam."

"That sounds like a wonderful way to spend your day," says Mom.

"There's more," I say. "I want to take

a bubble bath and paint my toenails."

"Ugh!" says Max like he's heard enough. He stands up. "Have fun resting and relaxing. I have to go to baseball practice." He grabs his duffel bag and walks toward the door.

When he's gone, I put some scrambled eggs and a slice of toast on my plate. I take a bit of eggs. Even though today is my day to rest and relax, there's something important I want to talk to my parents about.

I clear my throat like I want their attention. Mom and Dad look at me.

"I'm really glad I did the poetry slam, and I'm glad I babysat for Lucas and Jared too," I say. "But I'm also kind of relieved both things are over." I shrug and look down. "I feel kind of bad saying that, and I'm not sure why."

Mom and Dad give each other a look. "You know, Mallory, part of growing up is taking on new challenges and trying new things," says Mom. "It isn't always easy. You might even try something and find that you wish you hadn't committed to doing it."

I nod like I get what she's saying. But there's something I *don't* get. "That's just it. How do you know if you're going to like something?"

Mom hesitates like she's thinking about her answer before she says it. "You don't know what you'll like until you try it," she finally says. "But the more you learn about yourself, the easier it will be to figure out what you like and what you're able to do."

When Mom says that, I laugh. I can't help it. "It sounds like you read that in a textbook for parents."

Now it's Mom's turn to laugh. "There are some things you don't learn from a book," Mom says.

Dad smiles at Mom like he appreciates what she's saying, and then he smiles at me too. "Mallory, my grandfather used to always say, 'I'd rather be sorry for things I did than things I've never done.'"

I scratch my head to help me think. "You mean it's better to try something and find out you don't like it than not to try?"

Dad nods. "That's exactly what I mean."

"I get it," I say to Dad. "But what if you start doing something like babysitting and it takes more time than you thought it would and it makes it hard to do the other stuff you're supposed to be doing?"

"Part of growing up is learning how to juggle your responsibilities," says Dad.

"It's not always easy," says Mom. "But Dad and I are confident you'll do a good job making smart choices and learning how to balance your priorities."

I think about what both of my parents just said. They sound very parental, but even so, I like knowing that they have confidence in me. I'm sure Mom was right when she said it won't always be easy.

But I, Mallory McDonald, am up for the challenge.

MALLORY MCDONALD'S TOP TEN BABYSITTING TIPS

Babysitting is hard work, but it's also fun. I've learned a lot about what to do and what not to do. For example, making a schedule and sticking to it is a great idea!

But I've learned lots of other things too.

Here are some of my top tips to help you be a great babysitter!

TIP #1: DO ask the parents for a list of rules, and be sure to follow them. If the child starts to misbehave, you can remind him (or her) that his parents made the rules and that they expect him to follow them!

TIP #2: DO make sure you have a list of phone numbers where you can reach the parents if they leave the house. It's also a good idea to have a number for the child's doctor and a neighbor too. You should know what numbers to call in case of an emergency.

Important
Phone Numbers

Mother 740·555·0311
Father 614-555-0326
Pediatrician 555-1019
Poison Control 1-800-411-1013
Neighbor 614-555-0825

TIP #3: DO talk to the parents about their expectations of what they'd like you to do with their child. It's always nice to come up with some ideas of your own (especially if they are fun or educational). Bottom line: Make a plan and discuss it with the parents to make sure you're both on the same page.

TIP #4: DO check with the parents to see what foods a child can eat. You want to be sure you know of any allergies they might have and be sure to avoid those foods!

TIP #5: DO clean up before you leave. Make sure everything is put away. Toys should go back in the closet or in the toy box, and

be sure all crumbs and garbage go in the trash. Parents love to come home to a clean house!

TIP #6: DON'T fall asleep on the job! That seems pretty obvious, but babysitting takes lots of energy. Be sure to show up well rested!

TIP #7: DON'T talk on the phone or spend time on the computer when you are supposed to be babysitting. If you have a phone, put it away! The only person you should be paying attention to is the one you are babysitting.

TIP #8: DON'T give the child any medications or leave the house without the parents' permission. The child's safety is your #1 priority!

TIP #9: DON'T complain to parents about their kids. If you are having a hard time, it's a good idea to ask for advice about how to improve a situation instead of complaining.

TIP #10: DON'T forget to have fun and smile. Chances are good that if you enjoy what you're doing, the kids you are babysitting will like it too!

POETICALLY SPEAKING

When I was in third grade, my teacher Mrs. Daily taught us an expression:

"Some things are best left unsaid." That might be true, but I think some things are best said in a poem!

It was really fun to participate in the poetry slam at school. I know how hard it can be to pick a topic or find inspiration for your poem. But I learned that one of the best ways to write a good poem is to write about something that happens in your life. And don't worry if you're not sure what you want to write about. Try a few different ideas and keep an open mind. The right idea will come to you. I promise!

Even though Chloe Jennifer and I didn't win the poetry slam, it inspired me to

 write some more poems. Here's one of my favorites. The inspiration for it came from the day Chloe Jennifer and I helped Lucas and Jared make smiley face sandwiches.

I hope you have as much fun reading it as I had writing it.

BETWEEN THE BREAD
BY MALLORY MCDONALD

When it's time to decide what goes
    between the bread,

There's no need to worry or
    have sandwich-making dread!

It's time to get creative. Almost
    anything will do.

The only rule to follow: Your
    sandwich should taste good to you!

You can use turkey, roast beef, cheese,
    or ham.

Spread on mustard and mayo. Or try
    strawberry jam!

Pile on sprouts or raisins.
Add avocado slices.

Sprinkle on salt and pepper.
Experiment with spices!

Some people like tomatoes, apple chunks, or grapes.

Others like bananas (and not just monkeys or apes!).

My favorite is peanut butter, with marshmallow creme or jelly.

Max prefers tuna fish! (To me, it's kind of smelly.)

My dad is a fan of hot dogs. He eats them all the time.

My mom likes chicken salad with pistachios and lime?!?

Everyone is different. Their favorite sandwich is too.

So when you pull out the bread, just decide,

What works for you?

I hope you enjoyed the poem. Try writing your own. It's a lot of fun. I promise. And if you get hungry while you're writing, you can always make yourself a sandwich!

Text copyright © 2017 by Laurie B. Friedman
Illustrations copyright © 2017 by Lerner Publishing Group, Inc.

Darby Creek
A division of Lerner Publishing Group, Inc.
241 First Avenue North
Minneapolis, MN 55401 USA

For reading levels and more information, look up this title at
www.lernerbooks.com.

Cover background images: © iStockphoto.com/Sonya_illustration (pencils);
© iStockphoto.com/NI QIN (scribble); © iStockphoto.com/FaberrInk (color bands).

Main body text set in LumarcLL 14/20. Typeface provided by Linotype.

Library of Congress Cataloging-in-Publication Data

Names: Friedman, Laurie B., 1964- author. | Kalis, Jennifer, illustrator.
Title: Mallory McDonald, super sitter / by Laurie Friedman ; illustrations by
    Jennifer Kalis.
Description: Minneapolis : Darby Creek, [2017] | Summary: "Mallory takes on a
    babysitting job, only to discover that it is more work than she expected
    and that she will have to learn to balance her commitments"— Provided
    by publisher.
Identifiers: LCCN 2016002665 (print) | LCCN 2016026812 (ebook) |
    ISBN 9781467750318 (th : alk. paper) | ISBN 9781512426960 (eb pdf)
Subjects: | CYAC: Babysitters—Fiction. | Responsibility—Fiction.
Classification: LCC PZ7.F89773 Mahj 2017 (print) | LCC PZ7.F89773 (ebook) |
    DDC [Fic]—dc23

LC record available at https://lccn.loc.gov/2016002665

Manufactured in the United States of America
2-43787-17189-9/21/2017